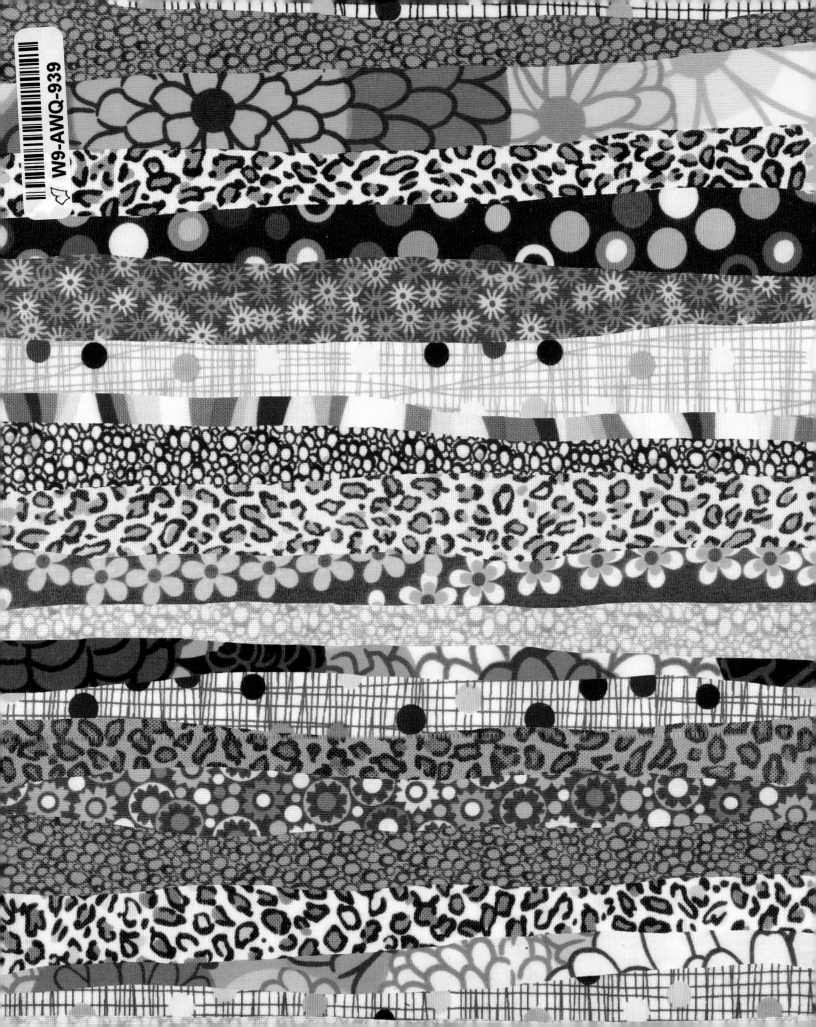

For Heather

Little, Brown and Company * Hachette Book Group * 237 Park Avenue, New York, NY 10017 * Visit our website at www.lb-kids.com

Little, Brown and Company is a division of Hachette Book Group, Inc. The Little, Brown name and logo are trademarks of Hachette Book Group, Inc.

First Edition: May 2011

All fabric prints modeled by Chamelia are courtesy and property of Alexander Henry Fabrics, Inc. www.ahfabrics.com

Library of Congress Cataloging-in-Publication Data * Long, Ethan. * Chamelia / by Ethan Long. — 1st ed. * p. cm. * Summary: Chamelia loves to stand out and often wears outrageous outfits, but eventually she learns to shine in other ways. * ISBN 978-0-316-08612-7 * [1. Individuality—Fiction. 2. Clothing and dress—Fiction. 3. Chameleons—Fiction.] I. Title. * PZ7.L8453Ch 2011 * [E]—dc22 * 201001975 2

10 9 8 7 6 5 4 3 2 *SC *Printed in China

The illustrations for this book were done in digital collage.
The text and display type are set in Barcelona.

Chamelia

by Ethan Long

Little, Brown and Company
New York   Boston

Most chameleons like to blend in.

But not Chamelia.

When others zig . . . .

Chamelia zags.

When others twist, Chamelia shouts.

When others rock, Chamelia rolls . . .

but in her own special way.

Sometimes, figuring out how to stand out can be difficult. . . .

So Chamelia makes sure she's ready for every occasion.

She wants to start every morning in a special way.

RIIIIP!

But sometimes things don't go as planned.

Her costume for the school play isn't quite right.

And apparently sequins and soccer don't mix.

TWEEEET!

Now, instead of standing out, Chamelia just feels *left* out.

But Chamelia's parents say standing out isn't the only way to feel special. Joining in can be just as fun!

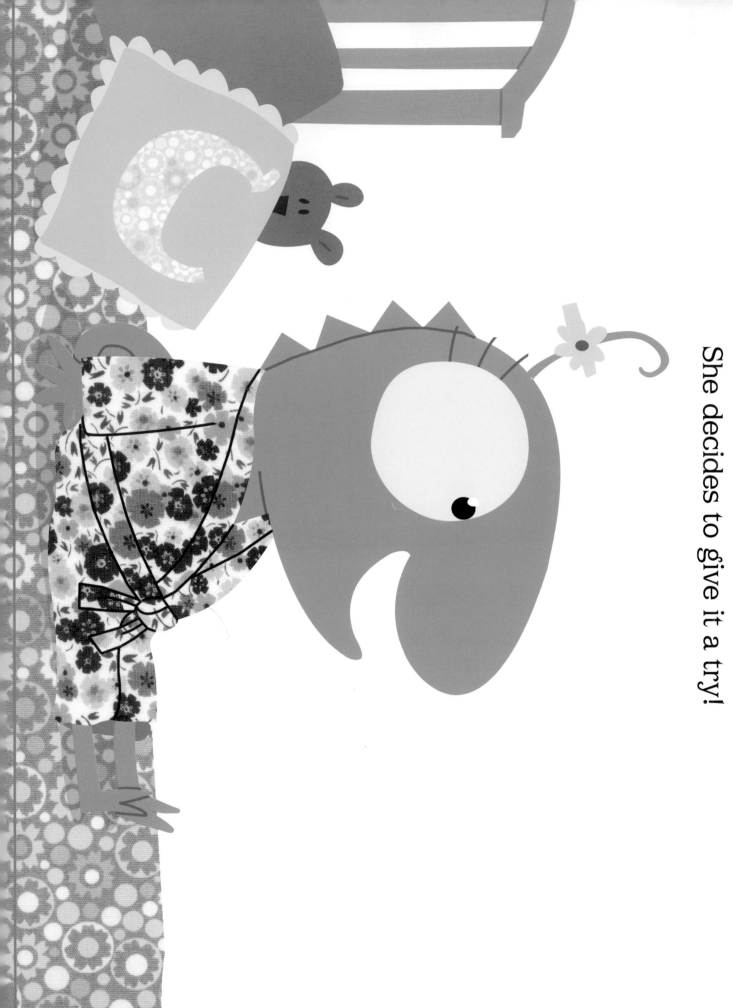

Chamelia wonders if there's a way to join in *and* be herself.
She decides to give it a try!

Now, even when Chamelia blends in . . . .

. . . . she knows she can always find a way
to make herself stand out.

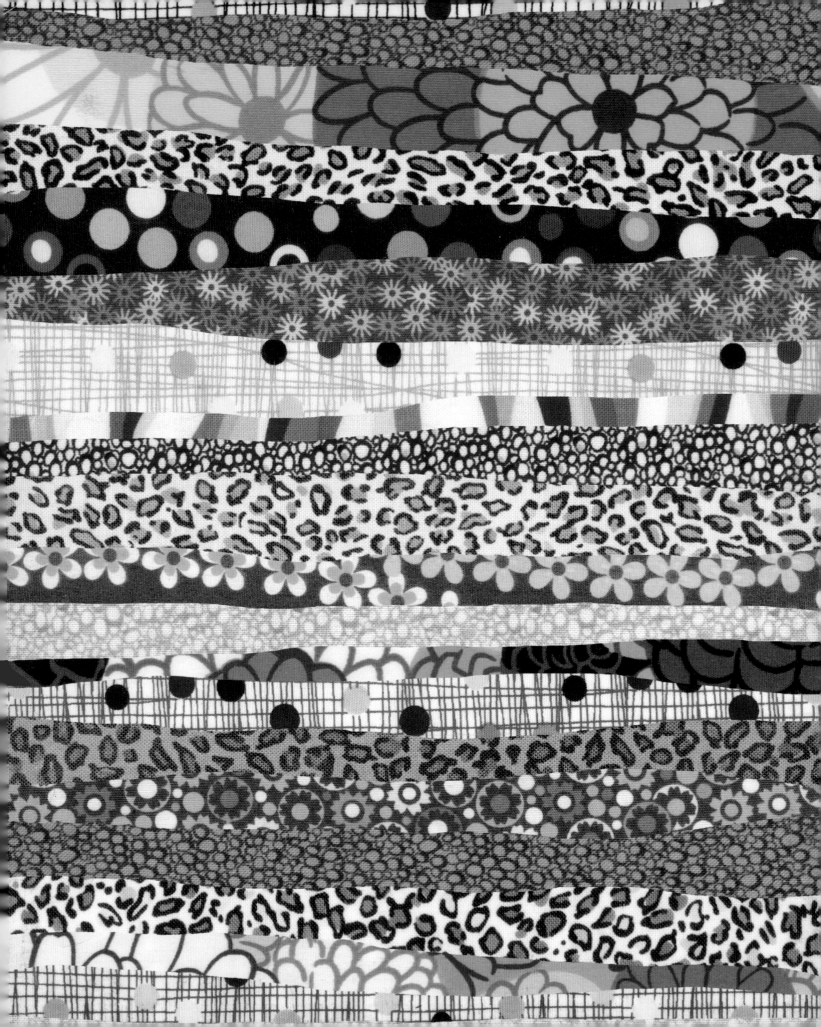